Farshore

First published in Great Britain by Farshore

An imprint of HarperCollins*Publishers*
1 London Bridge Street, London SE1 9GF
www.farshore.co.uk

HarperCollins*Publishers*
1st Floor, Watermarque Building, Ringsend Road
Dublin 4, Ireland

Licensed by:

ISBN 978 0 7555 0104 5
Printed in Romania
001

A CIP catalogue record for this title is available from the British Library.

Parental guidance is advised for the recipe and craft activity within the book. Always ask an adult to help when using glue, paint and scissors. Wear protective clothing and cover surfaces to avoid staining.

Stay safe online. Farshore is not responsible for content hosted by third parties.

Farshore takes its responsibility to the planet and its inhabitants very seriously.
We aim to use papers from well-managed forests run by responsible suppliers.

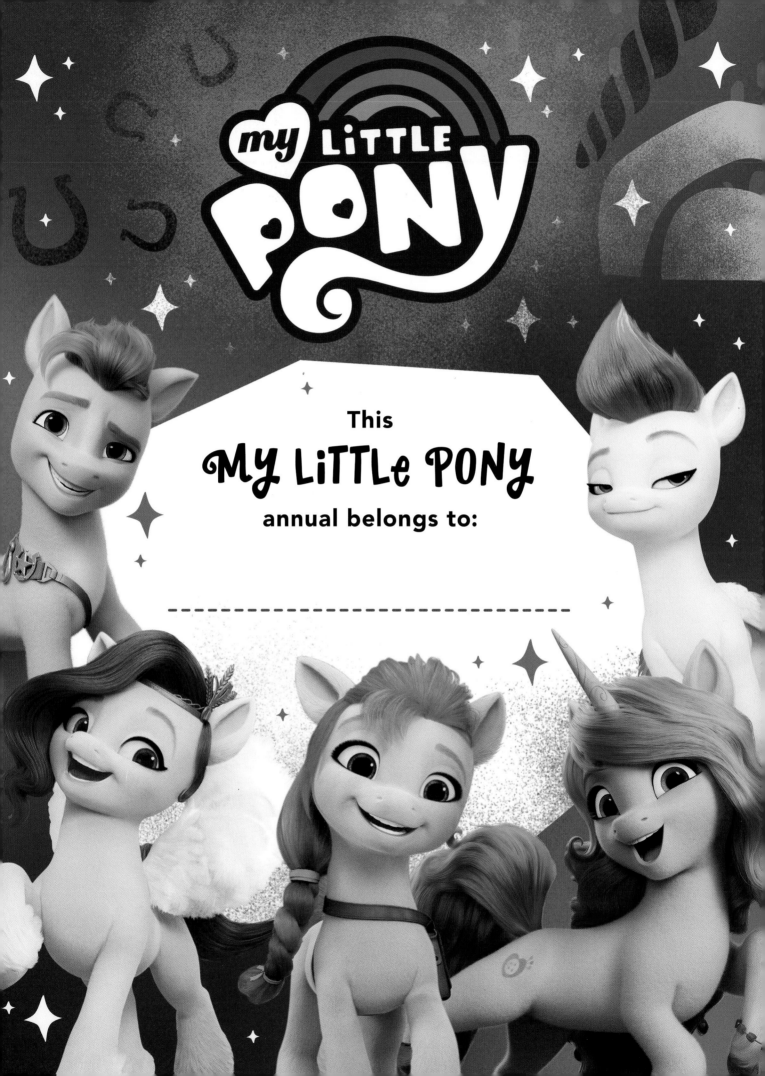

This
MY LITTLE PONY
annual belongs to:

WHAT'S INSIDE

ONCE UPON A TIME P8

CRACK THE CODE P9

TWILIGHT SPARKLE P10

PINKIE PIE P12

APPLEJACK P14

RARITY P16

FLUTTERSHY P18

RAINBOW DASH P20

FRIENDS IN EQUESTRIA P22

SCHOOL OF FRIENDSHIP P24

MEET THE VILLAINS P26

FIND QUEEN CHRYSALIS P27

CROWNING CONFUSION P28

COSTUMES CROSSWORD P29

FRIENDSHIP JOURNAL P30

MEMORY CHALLENGE P32

POSTERS P33

MEET SUNNY..P36

THE GUARDIANS OF HARMONY.............................P37

STORY: MARETIME BAY..................................P38

WELCOME TO MARETIME BAY..............................P40

LIGHTHOUSE LOOKOUT....................................P41

STORY: IZZY'S ARRIVAL................................P42

MEET IZZY...P44

JOURNEY TO ZEPHYR HEIGHTS............................P45

STORY: ZEPHYR HEIGHTS................................P46

MEET THE ROYAL PRINCESSES............................P48

ZIPP'S TANGLE MAZE...................................P50

PRINCESS PIPP'S PUZZLES..............................P51

STORY: BRIDLEWOOD....................................P52

BRIGHTEN UP BRIDLEWOOD...............................P54

ALPHABITTLE'S PUZZLE.................................P55

CRAFTING WITH IZZY...................................P56

STORY: THE FINAL CRYSTAL.............................P58

SPROUT'S SPOT THE DIFFERENCE.........................P60

STORY: MAGIC RETURNS!................................P62

WHICH PONY ARE YOU?..................................P64

QUIZ OF THE MOVIE....................................P66

ANSWERS..P68

ONCe UPON A TiMe . . .

Once upon a time, in the land of Equestria, there lived a bright unicorn named Twilight Sparkle. One day, she was given a very special assignment by Princess Celestia, ruler of Equestria: to learn about friendship.

Twilight Sparkle journeyed to Ponyville and met five ponies: Pinkie Pie, Applejack, Rainbow Dash, Fluttershy and Rarity. They became the best of friends … and together, they showed everypony the magic of friendship.

Equestria flourished, and Twilight Sparkle became the Princess of Friendship. All three pony kinds – Earth Ponies, Pegasus Ponies and Unicorns – lived in harmony.

CRACK THE CODE

Use the key below to find out the name of Twilight Sparkle's castle.

1	2	3	4	5	6	7	8	9	10	11
A	B	C	D	e	F	G	H	i	J	k

12	13	14	15	16	17	18	19
L	M	N	O	P	Q	R	S

20	21	22	23	24	25	26
T	U	V	W	X	y	Z

20	8	5

3	1	19	20	12	5		15	6

6	18	9	5	14	4	19	8	9	16

Answer is on page 68.

TWILIGHT SPARKLE

SPECIES: Alicorn
ELEMENT OF HARMONY: Magic
CUTIE MARK: Star

Twilight Sparkle has come a long way from the shy unicorn who preferred studying to spending time with friends. With the support of Spike the Dragon and her new pony friends, she settles into Ponyville, opens the School of Friendship and even becomes the fourth princess of Equestria!

Twilight Sparkle is extremely gifted at magic. After solving Star Swirl the Bearded's unfinished spell, she gets her wings and becomes an Alicorn. Twilight Sparkle defeated Queen Chrysalis, Dark King Sombra and Lord Tirek. Just don't introduce her to a ladybird.

"STAR POWER!"

10

Twilight Sparkle is the Protector of Equestria and the Princess of Friendship. Her friends know she is a great leader who can organise anything.

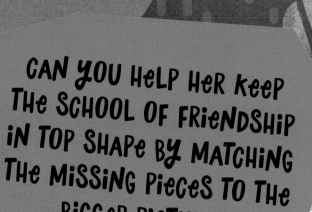

CAN YOU HELP HER KEEP THE SCHOOL OF FRIENDSHIP IN TOP SHAPE BY MATCHING THE MISSING PIECES TO THE BIGGER PICTURE?

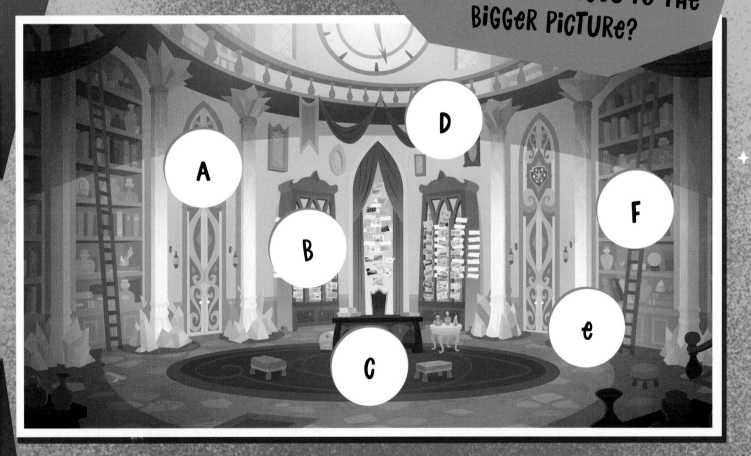

Answer is on page 68.

BRIDLE GOSSIP:
PinKie Pie

SPeCieS: Earth Pony
eLeMeNT OF HARMONY: Laughter
CUTie MARK: Three balloons

Pinkamena Diane Pie grew up on a rock with her sisters. When Rainbow Dash's sonic rainboom makes her smile, she realises her purpose in life is to spread joy and make everypony laugh. She sings in the face of monstrous visions, and makes peace between the Ponies and Yaks – and Prince Rutherford even makes her an honorary Yak.

Pinkie Pie loves to throw a good party. Has she mentioned her party cannon? But just don't ask her to keep a secret.

"FRee HUGS!"

Pinkie Pie is a cheerful pony who loves to make her friends smile, whether by telling silly jokes, throwing parties or baking delicious cakes in her bakery.

NOW YOU CAN MAKE THESE YUMMY CUPCAKES JUST LIKE PINKIE PIE!

ASK A GROWN-UP TO HELP YOU!

YOU WILL NEED:

90g unsalted butter, softened

100g white sugar

1 egg

1 tsp milk

1 tsp vanilla extract

120g self-raising flour

1 tsp baking powder

A pinch of salt

Icing or fruit for decorations

A wooden spoon

A mixing bowl

A cupcake tin

12 paper cases

1 Preheat the oven to 180°C / Gas mark 4. Line a cupcake tin with paper cases.

2 Mix the butter and sugar together until combined.

3 Add the egg, milk and vanilla, and stir well.

4 Add the flour, baking powder and salt. Mix until the batter is smooth.

5 Spoon the mixture evenly into 12 paper cases.

6 Ask an adult to put the cupcakes in the oven. Bake for 18–20 minutes, or until light golden and firm to the touch.

7 Leave to cool for 10 minutes, and then

DECORATE!

APPLEJACK

SPeCieS: Earth Pony
eLeMeNT OF HARMONY: Honesty
CUTie MARK: Three apples

Applejack loves her friends and she loves her family – the Apple family is the largest family in all of Equestria! Working on the family farm keeps her very busy, whether it's tending to crops and animals, baking apple fritters or preparing for the Helping Hooves music festival.

Applejack is always happy to work hard and get muddy – but sometimes her friends have to remind her that it's OK to ask for help or to take time to herself to enjoy a trip to the Ponyville Day Spa!

"HOWDY, PARTNeR!"

Applejack is a trustworthy pony who always comes through for her friends. She lives on Sweet Apple Acres with her family, and she loves to make apple cider!

CAN YOU HELP APPLEJACK THROUGH THE ORCHARD? PUT YOUR FINGER ON THE START, THEN TRACE A PATH THROUGH THE APPLES WITH AN EVEN NUMBER OF PIPS!

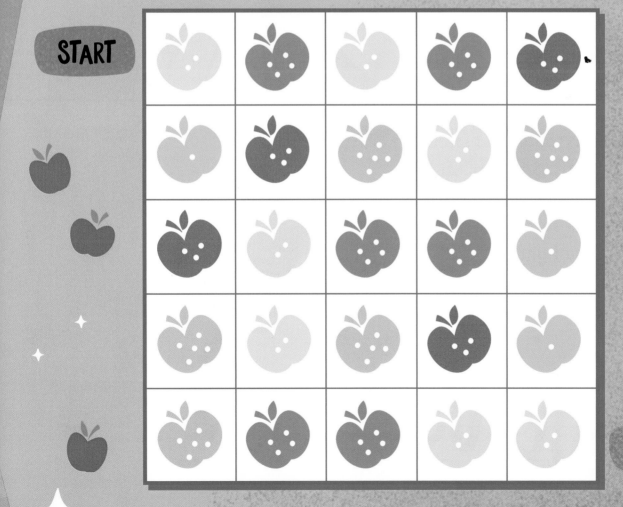

START

FINISH

Answer is on page 68.

RARITY

SPECIES: Unicorn
ELEMENT OF HARMONY: Generosity
CUTIE MARK: Three diamonds

After many years in Equestria designing fabulous dresses, Rarity enters a fashion competition and goes on to open a fashion boutique in Canterlot. She helps rescue the community theatre in Manehatten, and designs many marvellous costumes.

Rarity may be elegant, but she's not afraid to be tough and stand up for her friends. She cuts off her own tail to help out a sea serpent, and she defeats several changelings in a fight. But she is not impressed by bad manners.

"FABULOUS!"

Rarity is a kind-hearted unicorn who always looks dazzling. With lots of creativity and unicorn magic, she designs wonderful outfits for her friends to wear.

USE YOUR BRIGHTEST AND MOST SPARKLING COLOURS TO HELP RARITY LOOK SIMPLY FABULOUS!

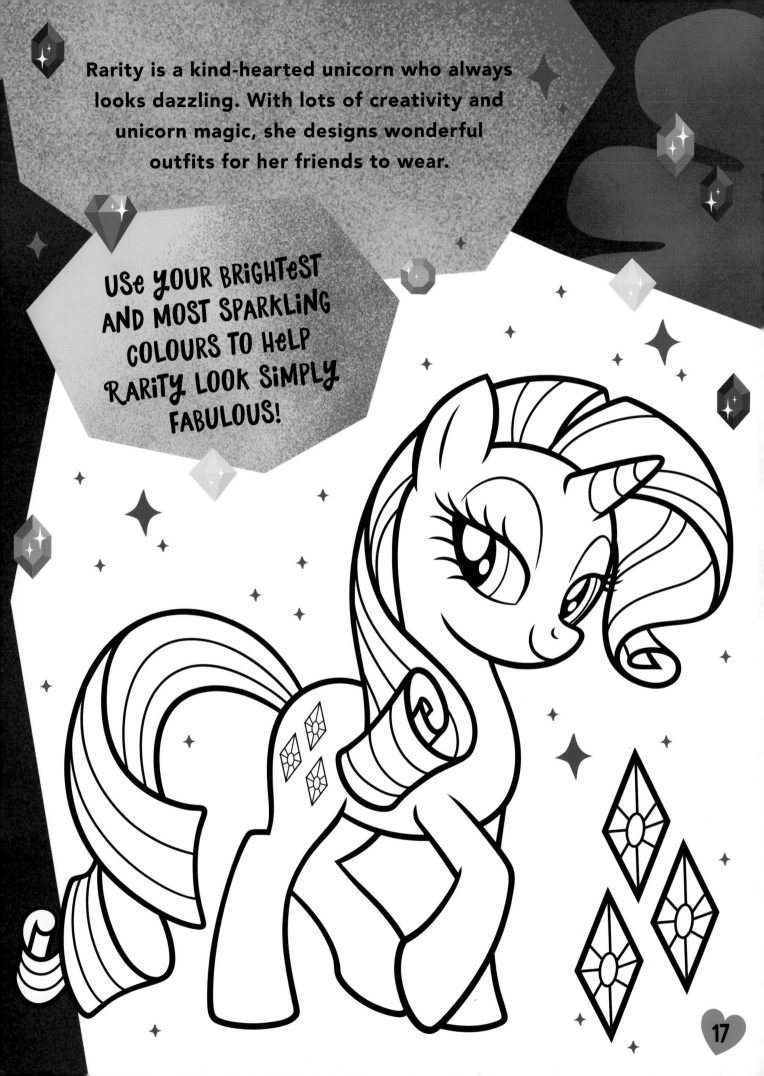

BRIDLE GOSSIP:
FLUTTERSHY

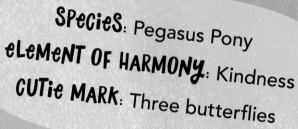

SPECieS: Pegasus Pony
eLeMeNT OF HARMONY: Kindness
CUTie MARK: Three butterflies

When Fluttershy first met Twilight Sparkle, she was too shy to say anything ... until she saw Spike. Sometimes she finds it easier to talk to animals! Fluttershy has built an animal sanctuary, and she leads a choir of woodland animals.

Though Fluttershy is quiet, she's not afraid to show compassion to even the fiercest foes like the manticore and Discord. And she'll stare down a full-grown dragon if it means standing up for her friends!

"FLUTTeR ON!"

Fluttershy is a sweet and thoughtful pony. She lives in a cottage at the edge of The Everfree Forest, and she loves caring for all the wildlife. She can even talk to the animals!

CAN YOU HELP FLUTTERSHY MATCH UP SEVEN PAIRS OF ANIMALS AND FIND ONE LEFT OVER?

WHICH ANIMAL DOESN'T HAVE A PAIR?

Answer is on page 68.

19

RAINBOW DASH

SPECIES: Pegasus Pony
ELEMENT OF HARMONY: Loyalty
CUTIE MARK: Rainbow-coloured lightning

Rainbow Dash is a world-class athlete who performed her first sonic rainboom as a young filly. She moves at hypersonic speeds, and she can clear the sky of clouds in ten seconds flat. She can even generate a tornado when it's needed to clear the parasprites.

Rainbow Dash loves to compete, and she is part of the Wonderbolts elite flying squad. Though she always pushes herself to be the best, she loves her friends more than winning. Even if it means being beaten by Applejack in a game of horseshoes!

"20% COOLER!"

20

Rainbow Dash is loyal, brave and competitive. When she's not racing her friends, she helps look after the weather and keeps the skies clear.

CAN YOU HELP RAINBOW DASH THROUGH THE CLOUD MAZE TO REACH THE WEATHER FACTORY? GO AS FAST AS YOU CAN... RAINBOW DASH LOVES FLYING QUICKLY!

START

FINISH

Answer is on page 68.

FRIENDS IN EQUESTRIA

Equestria is home to lots of magical creatures and friends of Twilight Sparkle!

PRINCESS CELESTIA

A ruler of Equestria and Twilight Sparkle's teacher

PRINCESS LUNA

A ruler of Equestria and Princess Celestia's younger sister

PRINCESS CADANCE

Ruler of the Crystal Empire

SHINING ARMOR

Captain of the Canterlot Royal Guard

STARLIGHT GLIMMER

Twilight Sparkle's first friendship student

TRIXIE LULAMOON

A unicorn and travelling magician

SPIKE

A baby dragon and Twilight Sparkle's number one assistant

DISCORD

A Draconequus and loyal friend, although he loves chaos!

Can you find all 14 names hidden in the word search? Names read across, down and diagonally!

APPLEJACK

DISCORD

FLUTTERSHY

PINKIE PIE

PRINCESS CADANCE

PRINCESS CELESTIA

PRINCESS LUNA

RAINBOW DASH

RARITY

SHINING ARMOR

SPIKE

STARLIGHT GLIMMER

TRIXIE LULAMOON

TWILIGHT SPARKLE

R	A	I	N	B	O	W	D	A	S	H	P
P	P	T	S	N	S	P	A	P	A	L	R
C	R	W	T	P	H	E	Y	P	S	T	I
D	I	I	A	R	I	C	R	L	L	A	N
T	N	L	R	I	N	K	A	E	P	S	C
R	C	I	L	N	I	R	E	J	K	F	E
I	E	G	I	C	N	Y	D	A	M	L	S
X	S	H	G	E	G	B	I	C	K	U	S
I	S	T	H	S	A	D	S	K	E	T	C
E	C	S	T	S	R	I	C	O	D	T	A
L	E	P	G	L	M	A	O	D	L	E	D
U	L	A	L	U	O	A	R	W	G	R	A
L	E	R	I	N	R	R	D	I	L	S	N
A	S	K	M	A	R	I	M	Z	T	H	C
M	T	L	M	R	O	R	N	A	S	Y	E
O	I	E	E	M	F	D	A	S	W	M	A
O	A	O	R	N	S	H	A	P	Q	E	S
N	P	I	N	K	I	E	P	I	E	R	T

Answer is on page 68.

23

SCHOOL OF FRIENDSHIP

Twilight Sparkle and her friends set up the
School of Friendship to help every creature
learn about the magic of friendship!

1

WHAT IS YOUR FAVOURITE
SUBJECT AT SCHOOL?

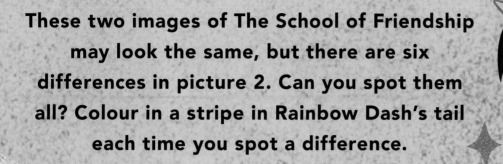

These two images of The School of Friendship may look the same, but there are six differences in picture 2. Can you spot them all? Colour in a stripe in Rainbow Dash's tail each time you spot a difference.

Answer is on page 68.

Meet The VILLAINS

Full of dark dreams and evil schemes, these villains love to cause chaos in Equestria!

SHADOW MATCH

Can you help Twilight Sparkle and her friends stop the forces of evil by matching the villains to their shadows?

A

B

C

D

e

1

2

3

4

5

FIND QUEEN CHRYSALIS

Queen Chrysalis can shape-shift into any creature. Can you pick out the real Chrysalis from the look-a-likes below?

A

B

C

D

Answers are on page 68.

CROWNING CONFUSION

Help Twilight Sparkle get everything in order for her crowning! Number the jumbled pieces from 1 to 6 to complete the scene.

28

Answer is on page 69.

COSTUMES CROSSWORD

Read the clues to crack the crossword and figure out which pony is wearing which dazzling disguise. Use the pictures to help!

1. This pony is dressed like Star Swirl. (8, 7)

2. This pony is wearing a silly chicken costume! (6, 3)

3. This pony is dressed up as Zapp to help defeat Mane-iac. (7,4)

4. This pony is wearing a secret spy disguise. (10)

5. This pony looks fabulous in her Grand Galloping Gala gown. (6)

6. This pony is wearing a scarecrow costume! (9)

Answer is on page 69.

FRiENDSHIP JOURNAL

Twilight Sparkle keeps a Friendship Journal.
Now you can write down some of your
favourite friendship stories and memories!

MY NAME iS: _____

MY BEST FRIENDS ARE: _____

OUR FAVOURITE GAMES TO PLAY ARE:

_____

_____

OUR FAVOURITE THiNGS TO EAT ARE:

_____

_____

WHEN I'M SAD, MY FRIENDS
MAKE ME FEEL BETTER BY:

MY FAVOURITE MEMORY OF MY FRIENDS IS WHEN:

NOW DRAW YOUR OWN
CUTIE MARK!

MEMORY CHALLENGE

Take a look at this picture, then cover
it up with a piece of paper. Now try and
answer the quiz questions below.
How much can you remember?

1 How many ponies are there?

2 Which pony is flying?

3 What colour is the tapestry?

4 True or false: Applejack is wearing a hat.

5 True or false: The carpet is green.

Answer is on page 69.

follow

Y♥UR
HEART

NEW MOVIE

It's time to make way for a whole new group of ponies in the new My Little Pony movie. They are here to stay and there are many more to come! After many years, Equestria has become a very different place and the ponies must fight for friendship and harmony once more ...

Meet SUNNY

SUNNY STARSCOUT

Sunny is a determined and adventurous Earth Pony. She wants to make the world a better place, starting with restoring harmony between Earth Ponies, Unicorns and Pegasi. Sunny is never afraid to try new things!

"WE'LL DO OUR PART, HOOF TO HEART!"

THe GUARDiANS OF HARMONY

When Sunny was a young Earth Pony, her father told her stories about Ancient Equestria and Princess Twilight Sparkle. Together, Twilight Sparkle and her friends taught everypony about the magic of friendship. They were the Guardians of Harmony.

Sunny loved these stories about the olden times, when Earth Ponies, Unicorns and Pegasi all lived in peace. She dreamed of having a friend who could fly around or float things. Maybe she could figure out how to bring the magic of friendship back.

So she told her father:

"SOMeDAY, THe BOTH OF US WiLL MeeT UNiCORNS OR A PeGASUS, AND We'LL Be BeST FRieNDS FOReVeR!"

STORY:
MARETIME BAY

Sunny tried to share her father's stories with her friends, Hitch and Scout. She wanted to play 'Saving Equestria', just like Twilight Sparkle did.

But her friends didn't believe that Unicorns or Pegasi could be trusted. "My mum says that the Pegasi and Unicorns tried to eat up all the Earth Ponies," Sprout scoffed. "If they ever come back to Maretime Bay, we'll kick their butts again!"

Sunny knew she had to stand up for what she believed in. She was sure that all three pony kinds could be friends again. So one night, she wrote a letter:

DEAR UNICORNS AND PEGASI,
YOU HAVE FRIENDS IN MARETIME BAY.
COME VISIT US!

Her father helped her tie the letter to a paper lantern, and send it off into the starry sky.

As Sunny grew up, she kept trying to convince the other Earth Ponies that Unicorns and Pegasi should be welcome in Maretime Bay.

"Peace with ponies! Unity with unicorns!" Sunny cheered. "Aren't you tired of being scared all the time?"

Hitch tried to stop her. He was the Sheriff of Maretime Bay now, and didn't want Sunny to stir up any more trouble.

But Sunny hoped that one day, everything would change …

WELCOME TO MARETIME BAY

The charming seaside town Maretime Bay is the home of the Earth Ponies.

MEET

HITCH TRAILBLAZER

Hitch is the Sheriff of Maretime Bay, and foalhood friend of Sunny. Hitch wants everypony to follow the rules, but he is caring and kind to all. He has a squad of adorable critters that follow him around everywhere.

"I'M HERE TO KEEP EVERYPONY SAFE."

"THAT'S DEPUTY SPROUT TO YOU."

MEET

SPROUT

Sprout is the Deputy of Maretime Bay, and he's jealous of Hitch! His mother Phyllis is the founder of Canterlogic, a factory that makes accessories to keep Earth Ponies safe in case the Unicorns or Pegasi attack.

LIGHTHOUSE LOOKOUT

The old lighthouse on the edge of town is Sunny's home. Can you spot which of these six pictures is the odd one out?

A

B

C

D

e

F

Answer is on page 69.

IZZY'S ARRIVAL

One afternoon, Sunny was sitting all alone on a bench. She had spent the morning trying to convince the Earth Ponies that Unicorns weren't scary, but nopony would listen to her.

Suddenly, Sunny heard screams in the street. Ponies were running in all directions, looking terrified. And then Sheriff Hitch shouted:

"Unicorn attack! This is not a drill! I repeat, this is not a drill!"

But the Unicorn wasn't attacking anypony. She was smiling and waving. **"My name's Izzy!"** she called out.

Hitch ordered the Earth Ponies to set up their Unicorn traps. Before she realised what was happening, Izzy was captured!

Sunny knew she had to do something!
Quickly, she hit the lever to free Izzy. Sunny led
Izzy back to her lighthouse as fast as they could gallop.

When they were safely inside, Sunny and Izzy stared at each other
in wonder. Sunny had so many questions for Izzy! Where was she
from? Did she live in a tree? What pizza toppings did she like?

Izzy told Sunny all about the Unicorns of Bridlewood. Many,
many moons ago they all had magic, but it had disappeared. Izzy
thought it might have something to do with the Pegasi.

"I've got it!" Sunny cried.
They could go on a quest to
the Pegasus City of Zephyr
Heights to bring back the
Unicorns' magic ... and restore
harmony to all ponykinds!

Meet IZZY

IZZY MOONBOW

Izzy is a thoughtful, creative Unicorn from the enchanted forest of Bridlewood. She's full of kindness, energy ... and sparkle! Izzy loves playing games and wants to make lots of new friends when she comes to Maretime Bay.

"Hi, NEW FRIEND! MY NAME'S IZZY!"

JOURNEY TO ZEPHYR HEIGHTS

Help Sunny and Izzy find their way to Zephyr Heights. Watch out for Sheriff Hitch and Deputy Sprout!

START

FINISH

Answer is on page 69.

STORY:
ZePHYR HeiGHTS

At first, things didn't go so well in Zephry Heights. Two guards named Thunder and Zoom stopped Sunny and Izzy and brought them to the castle of Queen Haven, Princess Zipp and Princess Pipp.

The Queen thought Sunny and Izzy were there to ruin the Royal Celebration. She ordered the guards to take them to the dungeons.

But Princess Zipp believed them! She helped Sunny and Izzy escape. "I have to show you something," she said.

Zipp led them through a trap door. There was a stained-glass window from long ago, from before the magic disappeared.

Sunny had an idea! If they could put the Pegasus Crystal and Unicorn Crystal back together, the magic might return!

First, they needed the Pegasus Crystal in
Queen Haven's crown. So Izzy made a decoy
crown from macaroni, jellybeans and glitter. Sunny
switched the crowns during the Royal Concert while the
Queen was watching Princess Pipp singing. Everything was
going to plan!

What they didn't know was that Hitch had followed them from
Maretime Bay! He burst into the castle, and started chasing Sunny.
Suddenly, the whole Royal Celebration was in chaos!

Princess Pipp managed to grab the Pegasus Crystal, but now
the Royal Guards were after them! Pipp was furious that her
performance had been ruined, but Zipp convinced her they had
done the right thing.

"This might be our only
chance," Zipp explained,
as they escaped from
Zephyr Heights ...
**and started for
Bridlewood!**

The ROYAL PRINCESSES

PRINCESS ZIPP

Princess Zephryina "Zipp" Storm is daring, bold and super-cool. She'd rather race around the canyons and go on adventures than attend a royal ball. She may be tough, but she's a loyal friend who will never let anypony down.

"JUST CALL Me ZiPP."

PRINCESS PIPP

Princess Pipp Petals was born to shine!
She loves to sing, dance and perform
for her fanponies, the PippSqueaks.
Pipp is confident and kind and will stop
at nothing to help her friends!

"PiPP PiPP HOORAY!"

ZiPP'S TANGLe MaZe

Princess Zipp wishes she could fly. But since the magic disappeared, the Royal Family use wires to pretend. Follow the wires to find out which one leads to Zipp!

Answer is on page 69.

PRINCESS PIPP'S PUZZLES

All of Zephyr Heights is a stage for Princess Pipp! She loves to sing, and her fans can't wait to hear her latest song. Look at the puzzle below. Can you help Pipp find these sets of musical notes? They might be across or down. We've done the first one for you!

PIPP LOVES TO TAKE PHOTOS TO SHARE WITH HER FANS. CAN YOU WORK OUT WHO SHE HAS ZOOMED IN ON?

A   B   C   D

WHAT IS YOUR FAVOURITE SONG?

STORY: BRiDLeWOOD

The next morning, the friends arrived at the edge of Bridlewood Forest. Izzy led the way to her cottage. It was warm and cosy, with a big table for a tea party.

Sunny realised they would need to blend in while searching for a Unicorn Crystal. Izzy made everypony a fake horn to wear. "You're going to fit right in!" she said.

At the Crystal Tea Room, a Unicorn called Alphabittle had just the crystal they needed. But Alphabittle wasn't going to give up the Unicorn Crystal for free, so Sunny challenged him to a contest. Alphabittle smirked, and told Sunny it would be a dance-off!

"You've got this, Sunny!" Izzy called out.
"I believe in you!"

Sunny danced and spun, faster and
faster. Alphabittle couldn't keep up.

Sunny was the winner! But as she cheered, her
Unicorn disguise slipped off. The friends had to hurry away. As
they reached the edge of Bridlewood, they bumped into a very
cross Queen Haven. On their other side was an angry Alphabittle!

Everypony started arguing, and Sunny was caught in the middle.
She tried connecting the Pegasus Crystal to the Unicorn Crystal,
but nothing happened.

Sunny didn't know what else to do. If this didn't work, maybe
nothing could bring back the magic.

Sunny felt like she had let everypony down. She returned
the crystals, and she and Hitch walked sadly back to
Maretime Bay.

BRIGHTEN UP BRIDLEWOOD!

Bridlewood Forest was once a gleaming place. But today the Unicorns are frightened of magic. Can you help bring the sparkle back by adding your brightest colours to this picture?

ALPHABITTLE'S PUZZLE

Alphabittle Blossomforth loves solving tricky puzzles! Can you figure this one out? Match the pieces of this pony with the corresponding parts of his shadow.

Answer is on page 69.

CRAFTING WITH IZZY

Izzy loves craft projects. This super creative Unicorn is great at 'Unicycling' – making art from recycled items.

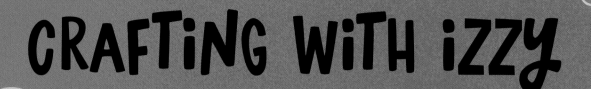

YOU CAN MAKE YOUR OWN PASTA PICTURES, JUST LIKE IZZY!

WHAT YOU NEED:

Coloured paper or card

Dried pasta shapes

Craft glue

Paint to decorate

Newspaper

(to protect your surface)

ASK AN ADULT TO HELP YOU!

WHAT TO DO:

Glue the pasta shapes to your piece of card or paper. You could make flowers, a rainbow, or a design of your own!

Let it sit until dry.

Now it's time to decorate your picture.

USE YOUR BRIGHTEST COLOURS!

WHY NOT ADD BUTTONS, YARN OR STICKERS TO MAKE YOUR PICTURE EVEN MORE SPECIAL!

THE FiNAL CRYSTAL

Back at home, Sunny collected her old Twilight Sparkle toys and threw them into a box. She felt silly for having thought she could fix things.

Suddenly, a shaft of light illuminated the room. It reminded Sunny of when she was little and her father would tell her stories about Ancient Equestria. And then Sunny noticed the crystal in her lantern. There was a third crystal – an Earth Pony Crystal! And if Sunny could put all three together, maybe she could finally restore magic!

Sunny ran to find Hitch and tell him!

58

But back in the Maretime Bay Sheriff's office,
Sprout was scheming.

Since Hitch had been away, Sprout had taken over.
"You're in charge now," his mother Phyllis told him.

Sprout told the other ponies stories about how the Unicorns
and Pegasi were coming for them. With the help of his mother,
he made everypony feel frightened.

"They're going to take over the village," Sprout said.
"We are all in danger!"

Sprout ordered the Earth Ponies to
build a giant battle machine called
Sprouticus Maximus. By the time
Sunny and Hitch arrived at
the Sheriff's office, Sprout
was already ordering the
ponies to attack!

SPROUT'S SPOT-THE-DIFFERENCE

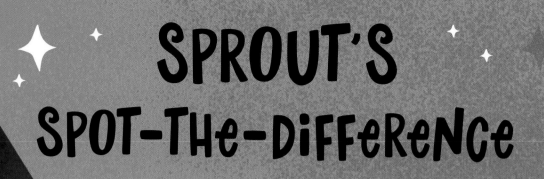

1

While Sunny and Hitch were away, Sprout convinced the Earth Ponies of Maretime Bay that they needed to prepare to attack! Can you spot the five differences in picture 2? Colour in a star each time you spot a difference.

2

Answer is on page 69.

STORY:
MAGIC RETURNS!

"Listen to me," Hitch called out. "The Pegasi and Unicorns can be our friends. There's no need to be afraid!"

"We can bring magic back!" Sunny added. "And bring *friendship* back!"

But Sprout was already driving the Sprouticus Maximus machine towards Bridlewood. Sunny and Hitch had to warn their friends!

Then Sunny saw somepony off in the distance. It was Izzy! With her were Pipp and Zipp. And behind them there was Queen Haven, Alphabittle and all the Unicorns and Pegasus Ponies **– together!**

Queen Haven explained that seeing the Princesses' friendship with Sunny and Izzy had made everypony realise that it wasn't too late to come together in harmony.

Before Sunny could connect the three crystals, the machine drove right into her lighthouse! The crystals were lost in the rubble.

Sunny's friends gathered round to help her. Then Sunny realised something very important: It wasn't the crystals that needed to come together. It was the Earth Ponies, Pegasi and Unicorns. And they were all coming together right now!

The crystals rose up from the ground. Then suddenly, rainbow beams filled the sky. Magic was restored! Izzy's horn started to glow. Pipp and Zipp's wings were sparkling. **They could fly for real now!**

The rainbow light lifted Sunny off the ground … and transformed her into an Alicorn, with her own Unicorn horn and Pegasus wings!

"You did it, Sunny," Hitch exclaimed.

"No," Sunny replied.

"WE DID IT TOGETHER!"

WHICH PONY ARE YOU?

Take this fun quiz to find out which character you're most like!

1

WHERE WOULD YOU LIKE TO LIVE?

a.   In a lighthouse by the sea.
b.   In a treehouse covered in twinkly lights.
c.   In a castle with a huge royal stage.
d.   Anywhere that isn't a fancy royal ballroom!

2

YOUR SPARKLE GLOWS BRIGHTEST WHEN YOU ARE DOING WHAT?

a.   It doesn't matter … as long as my friends are with me!
b.   Arts and crafts … with lots and lots of glitter!
c.   Performing my newest song in front of all my fans!
d.   Rock-climbing with a side of parkour.

3

WHAT IS YOUR DREAM JOB?

a.   Activist – so I can help make changes to make the world better.
b.   Artist – so I can create something funky and beautiful!
c.   Pop-star – so I can fill the world with music!
d.   Athlete – so I can play sports with my favourite teammates!

4 CHOOSE A CUTIE MARK:

a.   A star.
b.   A heart.
c.   A music note.
d.   A lightning bolt.

5 WHAT WOULD BE YOUR DREAM BIRTHDAY?

a.   A party with all your friends.
b.   Making your own pottery.
c.   A sold-out concert.
d.   An outdoor obstacle course.

MOSTLY A:

You're most like **Sunny**!

You are curious and optimistic, and always believe in your friends!

MOSTLY B:

You're most like **Izzy**!

You are creative and inventive, and you love a bit of sparkle!

MOSTLY C:

You're most like **Pipp**!

You are confident and charming, and you were born to be a star!

MOSTLY D:

You're most like **Zipp**!

You are brave and athletic, and always true to yourself!

QUIZ OF THE MOVIE

How well do you know the movie?
Take this fun quiz to find out!

1 WHERE DOES SUNNY LIVE?

a. Ponybeach
b. Maretime Bay
c. Ocean Heights

2 HOW DID SUNNY SEND HER LETTER OF FRIENDSHIP?

a. By boat
b. By pony post
c. By paper lantern

3 WHAT ARE THE NAMES OF THE PEGASI GUARDS?

a. Zoom and Thunder
b. Boom and Lightning
c. Doom and Cyclone

4 WHO PERFORMED AT THE ZEPHYR HEIGHTS ROYAL CONCERT?

a. Princess Zipp
b. Princess Pipp
c. Queen Haven

5 WHERE IS IZZY FROM?

a. Bridlewood
b. Fiery Forest
c. Magic Meadows

6 WHAT DOES ALPHABITTLE CHALLENGE SUNNY TO?

a. A trivia contest
b. A seven-legged race
c. A dance contest

7 WHERE DOES SUNNY FIND THE EARTH PONY CRYSTAL?

a. In the Sheriff's office
b. In the smoothie cart
c. In her lantern

8 WHAT DOES SUNNY BECOME AT THE END OF THE STORY?

a. A Unicorn
b. An Alicorn
c. A Pegasus Pony

Answer is on page 69.

ANSWeRS

PAGe 9:
The Castle of Friendship

PAGe 11:
1C; 2E; 3F; 4B; 5D; 6A.

PAGe 15:

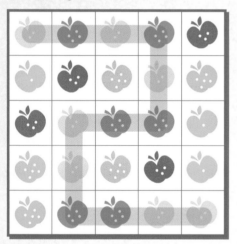

PAGe 19:
The squirrel doesn't have a pair.

PAGe 21:

PAGe 23:

PAGeS 24-25:

PAGe 26:
A4; B5; C3; D2; E1.

PAGe 27:
C is the real Queen Chrysalis.

PAGE 28:

5   2   4   6   3   1

PAGE 29:

PAGE 32:

1. There are 8 ponies.
2. Rainbow Dash is flying.
3. The tapestry is purple.
4. True.
5. False.

PAGE 41:

Picture D is the odd one out.

PAGE 45:

PAGE 50:

B is the correct line.

PAGE 51:

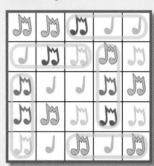

A is Queen Haven; B is Izzy; C is Zipp; D is Sunny.

PAGE 55:

A3; B2; C6; D4; E1; F5.

PAGES 60-61:

PAGES 66-67:

1B; 2C; 3A; 4B; 5A; 6C; 7C; 8B.